JOSEPHA

a prairie boy's story

STORY BY JIM McGUGAN   ILLUSTRATED BY MURRAY KIMBER

NORTHERN LIGHTS BOOKS FOR CHILDREN

RED DEER COLLEGE PRESS

It was late in the last afternoon, long after the school bell, when I made good-byes to Josepha.

Prairie wind ruffled his hair. Barefoot, he stood silent and still as a Saturday flagpole. The sun flickered between leaves in the windbreak poplars, licking his face in shadow and light. Shadow and light. And a farm cart's four wheels groaned and whined not far down the gravel track. A farm cart coming for Josepha.

Over the beating of my heart, I could hear them plain, drumming and churning inside my head. Josepha hummed the wagon's tune. He growled louder and louder as the wagon grew nearer and nearer. Then his eyes watered, and his breath gave out. And he coughed and laughed. And I laughed, too.

I tried to stretch up and clutch Josepha's elbow, but he broke free. And he reeled around me, clapping the gray dirt walk. Smacking the land with the soles of his naked feet. Wee slaps bouncing up from the ground, like the whack of Josepha's twine suspenders plucking against his bare back.

Rap rap tap. Josepha's slate ofttimes slipped onto the pine plank floor. Our schoolhouse floor. The floor way over in primary row. *Rap rap tap.* Red-faced Josepha. Past fourteen and trying to learn in primary row.

"Please, Josepha," Miss said. "Say it again."

To the newcomers, our words must have sounded like sheep talk. The younger children might fight to understand, but the older ones, never. When they braved to speak, they were made the fool.

As always, Josepha bore teasing with a smile. That last winter, though, someone dared to mock his sister. He reeled, then faced the class. I could smell his rage, and I was scared. Josepha quivered. But he could not say what he had to say.

He did not know how.

Later, Josepha wept. Miss sat by him until home time, resting her hand on his shoulder.

English speaking was the rule. Talk in English. Print in English. Think in English. Or sit with the little ones till you're able.

So silent Josepha sat with me.

And became my friend *for aye,* for always.

All hushed and muffled like a frozen river. A blushing bull in primary row. His final year in primary row.

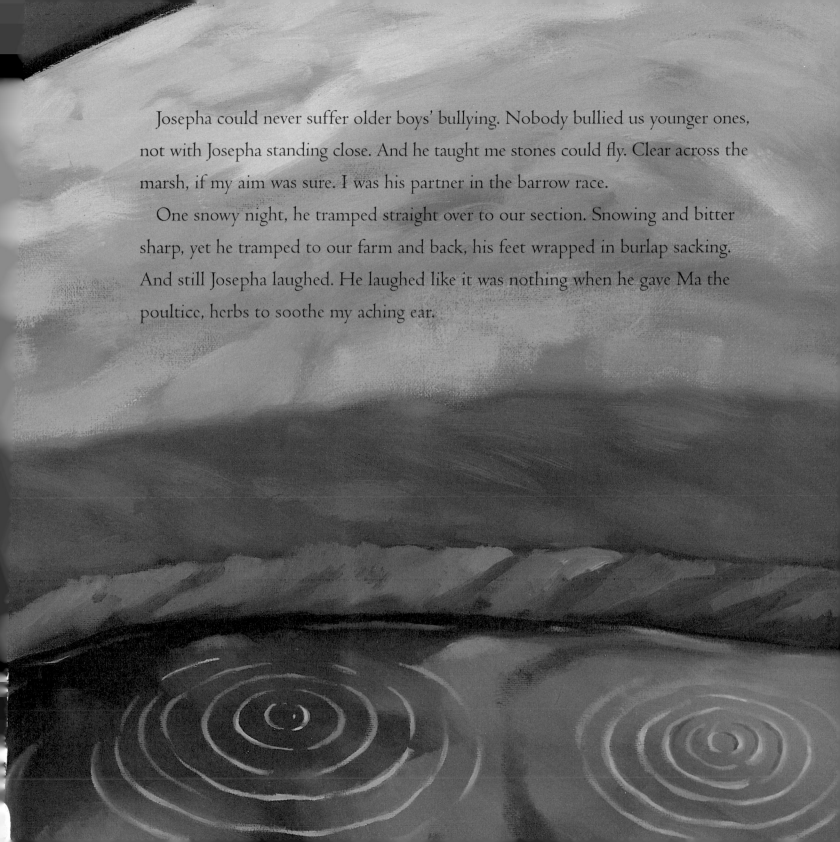

Josepha could never suffer older boys' bullying. Nobody bullied us younger ones, not with Josepha standing close. And he taught me stones could fly. Clear across the marsh, if my aim was sure. I was his partner in the barrow race.

One snowy night, he tramped straight over to our section. Snowing and bitter sharp, yet he tramped to our farm and back, his feet wrapped in burlap sacking. And still Josepha laughed. He laughed like it was nothing when he gave Ma the poultice, herbs to soothe my aching ear.

And now he tramped the land again. Tramping the land with the
bare soles of his feet.

"Dollar day. Dollar day. Dollar day a *baggink*."

He twirled about his sisters, jostling and jolting, jostling and jolting
because that's what you do. That's what you do if you have to laugh.
Jostling and jolting and rustling up clouds.

Yard dust powdered my boots, my brown boots with newspaper stuffed in the toes. They cost. They cost so much I didn't dare wear them except for very special times. Far too big and all, they were still the proudest thing I ever owned. And Josepha knew. When he saw the grit, his blue fold hankie rubbed and rubbed. And soon their leather toes shined again as bright as a birthday copper while I twitched and fussed, embarrassed.

Something dropped from his overall bib and lay tucked in the dirt.

A knife. Josepha's pocketknife. Josepha opened the blade and blew on the steel and returned it to its slot. He spun the handle around in place. One side goose-egg white, the other bare, its covering lost or broken. But the metal gleamed. He turned his knife over and over. I remembered whistles he'd carved. And I remembered dolls he'd given the littlest ones and arrows and bows for recess games. He spun the knife round and round.

Then jostling and jolting once more, he bumped into Miss. Our teacher. She made Josepha stop. And she asked him again.

"Please. Stay. Won't you stay, Josepha?"

She said his mind was soil rich and set to open. Like a flower to the sun, she said. She vowed he could learn. Come back after threshing, she said.

But Josepha's face darkened. Lightless as the window in his family's sod shack just after milking. You saw their home when you passed by at night from selling grain in town. A lonesome soddy standing on the rise, wee and frail and blackened. Supper in the gloom to save kerosene. Until next harvest. Or next. Pa said their storehouse was nothing but empty. And not a wonder, Pa said. For Josepha was the bairn of city folk, a main street shopkeeper's son. And Pa said Old Country or no, shopkeepers didn't make farmers. Farmers made farmers.

Josepha studied his teacher's eyes. He peered deep, his brow furrowing as if he were lost. Josepha sighed, then suddenly laughing, he said:

"Is dollar a day, Miss. *Baggink.*"

Eaton catalog English, we called it. Language enough for bagging grain through threshing time. Language enough to earn a one-dollar wage.

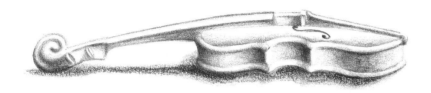

He smiled and pried ajar the lid of his biscuit tin. A meal pail for toting his boiled potatoes to school.

From inside he offered up a violin—a doll violin the span of a tanner's hand, whittled from a single shoot of cottonwood.

"For you, Miss. Is for you."

The gingham shoulders on Miss's dress sagged a mite before she stirred. She reached to accept her gift. But Josepha drew it back. He flashed his knife. In a glint, the blade pared the slightest burr from the neck of the violin.

And he placed the toy like a day-old chick into our teacher's hand.

She realized the work and wanted to protest, but didn't dare. To Josepha, a present offered must be taken.

Josepha's eldest brother reigned his wagon at the gate. Miss rubbed along the smoothness on the back of the violin with the edge of her thumb. She glared, angrily watching the old plow horse shake its leathers. The animal snorted, gnawing heads off some soft purple chicory clustered near the posts. And Miss brushed her thumb round and round and said:

"It is nineteen hundred. Nineteen hundred, Josepha. A fresh century in your chosen land. You are quick and bright and cunning. Oh, the wealth of knowing you could reap."

Josepha shrugged. Sheep talk. And Miss sighed.

This was the way for all of them, those older ones. One year, shamed. Maybe two. And then they'd be gone from class. They'd be gone forever.

"Best fortune, Josepha," Miss said. Then turning like a weather vane in a firebolt sky, she marched back to her empty school.

Josepha upped his sisters into the wagon.

And my forehead heated to a fever.

A gift. I could not think. I wanted to offer a gift to Josepha. A gift of his own for all the marvels he had given us. The wonders he had given me. I wanted to take his hand again. I wanted to beg.

Don't be quitting school, Josepha.

Instead, I watched him spring like a ram up alongside his brother in the cart.

He squeezed a buckboard sliver from his heel, then tossed down one last favor. Startled, I pressed his knife firmly to my chest.

"Josepha. Josepha, I've a thing to give as well." And so it was.

With a "Hrup, hup!" they were gone. Josepha shrinking smaller and smaller in the dust. And by the fork, he vanished into a hazy puff. Alone, I crossed the fallows home. I clutched the knife inside my fist. I wrung it greedily for memories.

Late in the last afternoon, trudging home.

Barefoot and pondering on Josepha.

Northern Lights Books for Children are published by
Red Deer College Press
56 Avenue & 32 Street Box 5005
Red Deer Alberta Canada T4N 5H5

Acknowledgements
Edited for the Press by Tim Wynne-Jones
Designed by Kunz & Associates Limited
Printed and bound in Korea for
Red Deer College Press.
The publishers gratefully acknowledge the financial assistance of
the Alberta Foundation for the Arts, the Canada Council, the
Department of Communications and Red Deer College.

Canadian Cataloguing in Publication Data
McGugan, Jim, 1948–
Josepha
(Northern lights books for children)
ISBN 0-88995-101-2
I. Kimber, Murray, 1964– II. Title. III. Series.
PS8575.G83J6 1993 jC813'.54 C93-091156-3
PZ7.M236Jo 1993

10 9 8 7 6 5 4 3 2 1